# THE
# THRONE
# OF FIRE

# THE THRONE OF FIRE

### THE GRAPHIC NOVEL

## RICK RIORDAN

Adapted and Illustrated by
**ORPHEUS COLLAR**

Additional
Illustration by
**CAM
FLOYD**

Color Flatting by
**ALADDIN
COLLAR**

Lettered by
**CHRIS
DICKEY**

**Disney • HYPERION**

Los Angeles  New York

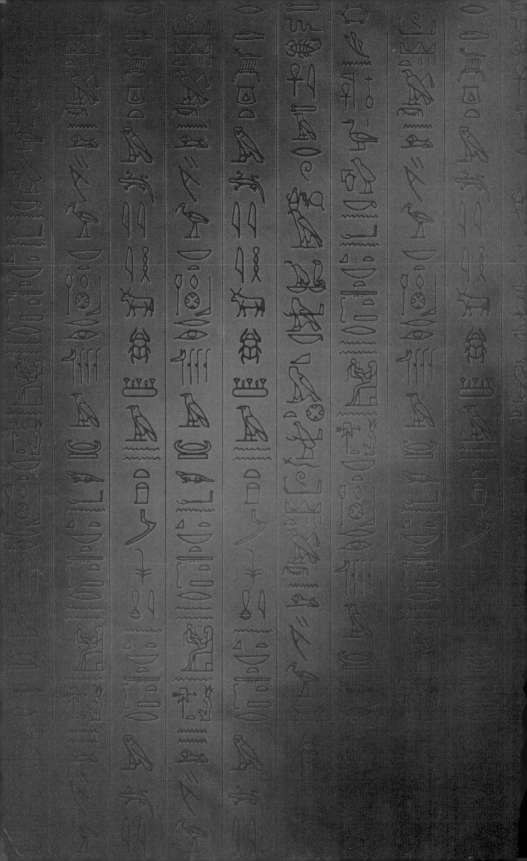

The job was supposed to be simple: sneak into the **Brooklyn Museum**, borrow a particular **Egyptian artifact**, and leave without getting caught.

No, it wasn't robbery. We would have returned the artifact eventually. But I guess we did look suspicious.

We had to try. We had to steal-- sorry, borrow--the artifact. Then we had five days to figure out how to use it. I just love deadlines.

Not to be dramatic, but the world was at stake!

# CHAPTER 1

Hi, Carter Kane here.

And I'm Sadie Kane.

We're siblings, even though we look nothing alike.

Last Christmas, we discovered we were **blood of the pharaoh** imbued with magical skills.

We used them to defeat the god of chaos **Set**, only to find he had been manipulated by a greater threat, **the serpent Apophis**, the entire time.

Last time we tried to save the world, we had the help of gods.

**Walt Stone** was our first trainee. The guy's a natural **sau--a charm maker.**

**Jaz** was a cheerleader from Nashville. She follows the path of the lion goddess Sekhmet, and is a natural healer.

**Khufu** is our pet baboon.

Since then, we've trained new magicians.

ALL CLEAR!

KHUFU, STAY UP THERE AND KEEP WATCH!

AGH!

What else? Let's see. The Egyptian gods are running around loose in the modern world; a bunch of magicians called the **House of Life** are trying to stop them; and a big snake is about to swallow the sun and destroy the world.

C'MON! THE EGYPTIAN WING IS THIS WAY.

THAT DOESN'T LOOK LIKE A *BOOK* TO ME. MORE LIKE A *MOOSE*.

IT'S NOT A MOOSE! *KHNUM* WAS ONE ASPECT OF THE SUN GOD.

AND WHO'S THE LITTLE GUY IN FRONT?

RA HAD THREE DIFFERENT PERSONALITIES. HE WAS *KHEPRI* THE SCARAB GOD IN THE MORNING; *RA* DURING THE DAY; AND *KHNUM*, THE RAM-HEADED GOD, AT SUNSET, WHEN HE WENT INTO THE UNDERWORLD.

THAT'S US! ACCORDING TO LEGEND, KHNUM MADE HUMANKIND FROM A POTTER'S WHEEL.

THIS STATUE SHOWS KHNUM CREATING A NEW LIFE.

MY HUNCH IS THIS IS WHERE WE'LL FIND THE SCROLL.

*I pulled out my wand.*

*W'PEH!*

*"Open!"*

SADIE, NO! IT MIGHT BE BOOBY--

--TRAPPED?

MISSION ACCOMPLISHED.

Jaz contained all the **bau** into a fissure in the ground.

But it was too much.

Her staff crumbled and she fell.

JAZ!!

...lt set his boat amulet on the ground and spoke the command word.

Voilà! Like one of those crazy expand-in-water sponge toys, the amulet grew into a full-size Egyptian reed boat.

With shaking hands, I took the two ends of the griffin's new necktie and tied one end to the boat's prow and one to the stern.

READY TO GO!

SADIE! HOW'S JAZ?

UM... NOT WELL!

*Jaz took something from her magician's bag--a wax figurine-- and pressed it into my free hand.*

YOU'LL NEED THIS SOON, SADIE. I'M SORRY I CAN'T HELP YOU MORE.

YOU'LL KNOW WHAT TO DO WHEN THE TIME COMES.

...

JAZ!

SADIE, WE NEED TO GET HER OUT OF HERE!

HEY! WHAT ARE YOU-- HEY! STOP!

GO! UP!

FREEEAK!

I steered the griffin toward our home.

To mortal eyes, **Brooklyn House** looked like a dilapidated warehouse down under the Manhattan Bridge.

But to magically trained eyes, the true form was revealed. Neat trick, eh?

GO! GET JAZ INSIDE. I CAN HANDLE THE GRIFFIN.

Carter's understanding of "handle the griffin" was different from mine, but I didn't say anything.

DOWN, BOY!

MEDIC!

WE NEED A HEALER!

Our initiates were an assortment of ages from around the world. Most were between ten and fifteen.

WHAT HAPPENED?

SOMEBODY GOT HURT?

The thing we all had in common: the blood of the pharaohs.

All of us were descended from Egypt's royal lines, which gave us a natural capacity for magic and hosting the power of the gods.

Felix was just nine. He'd shown a talent for summoning penguins and not much else...yet.

Sean, from Dublin.

Alyssa, from Carolina.

There was Julian, from Boston.

And Cleo, from Rio d Janeiro (yes, I know Cleo from Rio, but I not making it up!).

STILL BREATHING--

MAYBE THERE'S A SPELL IN THE LIBRARY...

LOOKS LIKE SOME KIND OF MAGICAL COMA!

AGH! OOO- AGH- AGH!

Khufu tried to revive Jaz with baboon mag without success.

IT'S NOT WORKING, KHUFU...

QUICK, LET'S GET HER TO THE INFIRMARY!

Poor Jaz. What had she slipped in my bag before passing out?

"You'll need this soon," she'd told me.

As far as I knew, Jaz was not a diviner. She couldn't tell the future. But she was a healer....

I recognized the likeness immediately. Jaz had crafted a figurine of Carter!

Based on its fine craftsmanship, I deduced it should only be saved for life-or-death situations.

Staring at the mini-Carter, I had a horrible feeling my brother's life had been quite literally placed in my hands.

BE CAREFUL WITH THAT, SADIE.

**?**

THE *BOOK OF RA* IS A DANGEROUS ARTIFACT.

OH, HI BAST.

...st knew a thing or two about Ra, having served as his battle ...c for thousands of years, fighting the serpent alongside him.

THE SCROLL SHOULD ONLY BE OPENED IN THE DAYLIGHT, WHEN THE POWER OF RA IS EASIER TO CONTROL.

WE'LL DISCUSS OVER BREAKFAST IN THE *MORNING.*

GET SOME SLEEP. YOU'VE GOT A *BIG DAY* TOMORROW.

*RIGHT.* THANKS FOR REMEMBERING.

Now she lived at Brooklyn House, as our resident cat goddess and adult chaperone.

GOOD GRIFFIN, SLEEPY GRIFFIN...IF YOU WANT TO CRASH HERE TONIGHT, WE CAN SET UP A *NEST* FOR YOU ON THE ROOF.

YAAWNN

When the sun rose tomorrow I'd be thirteen years old. Nothing like a birthday to put the impending apocalypse into perspective.

Before Carter sprung the Brooklyn Museum mission on us, I'd been making plans to celebrate my birthday in London. Now, I wasn't so sure.

At Brooklyn House, we sleep with magic charms to protect us against the occasional urge our souls--or **ba**, if you want to get Egyptian about it--get to wander out of our bodies.

Sometimes those calls are important, so I let my spirit go where it wanted to take me.

I found myself in a familiar underground chamber: the Hall of Ages, in the **House of Life's** main headquarters, under Cairo.

**The Hall of Ages** was so long, it could've hosted a marathon. Between its columns, curtains of light shimmered--holographic images from Egypt's history.

The light changed color to reflect different eras, from the gold glow of the Age of the Gods all the way to the crimson light of modern times.

At the end of the hall, seated at his post at the foot of the pharaoh's vacant throne, sat the leader of the House of Life, and my least favorite magician:

Michel Desjardins.

The last time I'd seen Monsieur Delightful, he threatened to execute Carter and me if we continued to break the House's most important law by interacting with gods of Egypt.

His face was gaunt. He studied the bloodred images in the curtains of light as if he were waiting for something.

?

The crimson tint of the modern age was darkening to a deep purple.

A NEW *AGE...*

...A *DARKER* AGE.

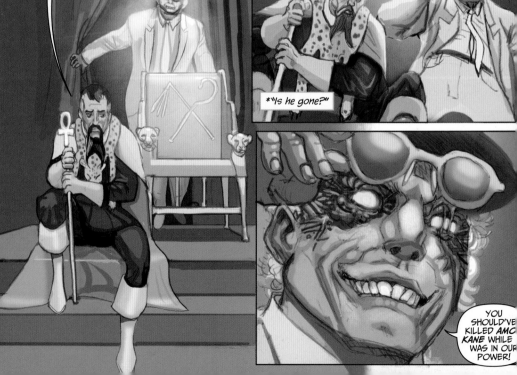

THE COLOR OF THE LIGHT HAS NOT CHANGED FOR A THOUSAND YEARS, VLADIMIR.

IT IS THE *KANES*, OF COURSE!

EST-IL ALLÉ?*

*"Is he gone?"

YES, MY LORD... HE USED THE PORTAL MOMENTS AGO. FINALLY, HE HAS GONE.

BUT IF YOU ASK ME...

YOU SHOULD'VE KILLED *AMO KANE* WHILE WAS IN OUR POWER!

NO, VLADIMIR. E WAS UNDER OUR PROTECTION.

ALL WHO SEEK HEALING MUST BE GIVEN SANCTUARY-- EVEN KANE.

BUT SURELY NOW THAT HE HAS LEFT, WE MUST ACT.

YOU HEARD THE NEWS FROM *BROOKLYN*, MY LORD. THE KANES ARE TEACHING THE *PATH OF THE GODS* TO A NEW GENERATION. AND NOW, THEY SEEK TO RAISE RA!

YES, VLADIMIR, BUT WE MUST USE OUR POWER TO KEEP DOWN THE SERPENT APOPHIS. BESIDES, THE KANES ONLY HAVE ONE SCROLL--THEY NEED THREE.

THE CHILDREN WILL SEEK THE OTHER SCROLLS, MY LORD. IF THEY LEAVE THEIR STRONGHOLD AND COME INTO MY TERRITORY--

I WILL LEAVE THAT MATTER TO YOU. THE SECOND SCROLL IS IN YOUR POSSESSION. YOU HAVE MY PERMISSION TO DISPOSE OF THE KANES SHOULD THEY SEEK TO STEAL IT.

EXCELLENT! BUT WHAT OF HEIR INITIATES IN BROOKLYN?

THEY HAVE LEARNED THE FORBIDDEN MAGIC OF THE GODS...AND HAVE LOYALTY TO THE KANES...

WE MUST *ATTACK* BEFORE THEY BECOME A STRONG FORCE AGAINST US.

ATTACK...

Desjardins turned to contemplate the swirling light of the new age, and my ba swirled into the currents of the Duat, back to my physical form.

It was morning. Time to see what could be done with the Book of Ra.

I WILL CHOOSE THE IME TO ATTACK, VLADIMIR.

NOW, LEAVE ME. I MUST THINK.

CHAPTER 2

RA'S PRIESTS CREATED THE *BOOK OF RA* IN ANCIENT TIMES AND KEPT IT SECRET, DIVIDING IT INTO THREE PARTS, TO REFLECT THE THREE ASPECTS OF RA--MORNING, NOON, AND NIGHT.

THE PIECES GRAFT TOGETHER. IT IS READABLE ONLY WHEN ALL THREE SECTIONS ARE JOINED.

THIS IS THE SCROLL OF KHNUM. YOU'LL NEED TO FIND THE OTHER TWO NOW.

I THINK I MAY HAVE A LEAD.

I HAD A TRIP LAST NIGHT IN THE HALL OF AGES.

DESJARDINS WAS CONSPIRING WITH A MAN WITH BURNT-OUT EYES.

*VLADIMIR,* I THINK HIS NAME WAS.

DESJARDINS TOLD VLADIMIR TO PROTECT THE SECOND SCROLL. IF WE CAN FIGURE OUT WHERE HIS STRONGHOLD IS, WE'D BE CLOSER TO WINNING.

WHAT EXACTLY HAPPENS IF APOPHIS ESCAPES?

APOPHIS WILL SWALLOW THE SUN.

ALL CIVILIZATION-- EVERYTHING HUMANS HAVE BUILT SINCE THE DAWN OF EGYPT-- WILL FREEZE OVER IN INFINITE DARKNESS AND BE REBORN IN THE IMAGE OF CHAOS.

THAT'S NOT ALL. VLADIMIR WANTED DESJARDINS TO ORGANIZE AN ASSAULT ON BROOKLYN HOUSE, TO KILL US... AND OUR INITIATES... FOR TEACHING THE PATH OF THE GODS.

IT SOUNDED LIKE A *SLAUGHTER.*

A wave of shock spread around the breakfast table as our initiates contemplated what it would mean to be attacked by experienced sorcerers many times their age.

SO... WE'RE ALL GOING TO DIE, THEN?

BUT... WE'RE NOT READY!!!

WE HAVEN'T BEEN FULLY TRAINED...

A light flashed behind Sadie and me as a familiar figure stepped through the portal.

INITIATES, BY THE TIME THE HOUSE OF LIFE ATTACKS, YOU *WILL* BE READY. EACH OF YOU.

UNCLE AMOS! YOU'RE BACK!

THAT I AM. I SEE YOU'VE RECRUITED!

LIN 17

It had been Amos's idea that we recruit in the first place. He did that before leaving for Egypt on his...

Hmm, what do you call it when someone goes for healing after being possessed by an evil god? Not a holiday, I suppose.

CHILDREN, I KNOW I'VE JUST ARRIVED, BUT I PROMISE WE'LL DO EVERYTHING WE CAN TO KEEP YOU SAFE.

I WILL OVERSEE YOUR TRAINING WHILE CARTER AND SADIE SEEK OUT THE REMAINING SCROLLS IN THE BOOK OF RA.

INITIATES, THIS IS OUR UNCLE AMOS. HE'S BEEN... STUDYING AT THE HOUSE OF LIFE.

SADIE, THE MAGICIAN YOU SAW IN YOUR VISION WAS NAMED *VLADIMIR MENSHIKOV*.

MENSHIKOV IS DESCENDED FROM THE *PRIESTS OF AMUN RA,* WHO WROTE THE BOOK OF RA. HE WAS ONCE A HERO OF THE HOUSE OF LIFE, BUT IN RECENT YEARS HIS BEHAVIOR HAS BECOME MORE... *CHAOTIC.*

MENSHIKOV ATTEMPTED TO ACCESS THE BOOK OF RA AND BURNED HIS EYES HORRIBLY IN THE PROCESS. HE CLAIMED HE WAS TRYING TO DESTROY IT, BUT I HAVE OTHER SUSPICIONS.

IT'S A MATTER OF PUBLIC RECORD WITHIN THE HOUSE OF LIFE THAT HE HOLDS THE SECOND SCROLL IN THE BOOK OF RA, THE SAME THAT DISFIGURED HIM.

MENSHIKOV'S TERRITORY, AND THE NEXT SCROLL, IS IN *ST. PETERSBURG,* RUSSIA.

IT'S BEST THAT YOU GET THERE SOON, BEFORE HIS DEFENSES INCREASE.

YOUR TIME IS LIMITED. THERE ARE *FOUR DAYS* BEFORE THE *SPRING EQUINOX,* WHEN THE HOURS OF DAY AND NIGHT ARE EXACTLY BALANCED, AND THE BALANCE OF *MA'AT** AND CHAOS CAN BE EASILY TIPPED ONE WAY OR ANOTHER.

*The order of the universe.

WE CAN'T WAIT TO ACT. THE EQUINOX IS ALSO THE PERFECT TIME FOR APOPHIS TO ESCAPE HIS PRISON AND INVADE THE MORTAL WORLD. YOU CAN BE SURE HE HAS *MINIONS* WORKING ON THAT RIGHT NOW.

SO IT'S A *TRIP TO RUSSIA,* THEN? I'LL GET PACKED. WE CAN LEAVE IN AN HOUR.

NO.

EXCUSE ME? WHAT WAS THAT, SADIE?

I SAID, NO! IT'S MY *BIRTHDAY*, AND I'M TAKING IT OFF.

I'VE BEEN PLANNING MY TRIP TO LONDON FOR AGES. THE BLOODY EQUINOX ISN'T FOR FOUR DAYS, AND BESIDES, IT'LL TAKE TIME FOR THE HOUSE OF LIFE TO PREPARE THEIR FORCES FOR AN ATTACK.

I THINK I HAVE TIME FOR ONE BLOODY DAY OFF BEFORE THE WORLD ENDS.

SADIE, A VISIT TO LONDON IS DANGEROUS.

HOWEVER, IF YOU MUST...

...THEN AT LEAST PROMISE YOU'LL BE CAREFUL. I DOUBT MENSHIKOV WILL BE READY TO MOVE AGAINST US SO QUICKLY.

YOU SHOULD BE ALL RIGHT IF YOU DO NOTHING TO ATTRACT ATTENTION.

AMOS!

I PROMISE!

THANK YOU, AMOS.

The initiates cleared the breakfast table, but I lingered behind. Couldn't Sadie see how selfish a London trip was?

I THINK THAT'S ENOUGH FOR ONE MORNING. WE WILL PREVAIL. WITH THE GODS ON OUR SIDE, MA'AT WILL OVERCOME CHAOS, AS IT ALWAYS HAS BEFORE.

THE MAIN THING IS FOR ALL OF YOU TO CONTINUE YOUR TRAINING. WE'LL NEED YOU IN TOP SHAPE TO DEFEND BROOKLYN HOUSE.

 RE YOU COMING O RUSSIA WITH US, BAST?

... NO. I WILL REMAIN HERE WITH AMOS TO PROTECT THE INITIATES FROM HARM. BUT I WON'T LEAVE YOU UNDEFENDED.

I'VE CONTACTED A *FRIEND* OF SORTS TO WATCH OVER YOU AND SADIE ON YOUR QUEST.

Sadie took the morning portal out to London, from our gateway on the roof, closing it for the next twelve hours.

I wanted to keep things as normal as possible for the trainees, so I led my usual morning class. I called it **Magic Problem-Solving 101**. The trainees called it "whatever works."

I gave the trainees a problem. They could solve it any way they wanted. As soon as they succeeded, they could go.

The training room took up most of the second floor. Aside from a nice collection of weapons, we'd tuck statues of Ra on the baseline walls and hollowed out their sun-disk crowns so we could use them as basketball hoops.

OKAY, GUYS. TODAY WE'LL START WITH A SIMPLE COMBAT SIMULATION.

SAPER!*

*"Miss!"

True to Alyssa's spell, her shabti missed every shot...

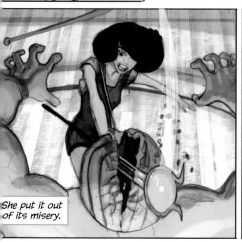

She put it out of its misery.

Felix went the simple and violent route.

YOU DIDN'T SAY WE HAD TO USE MAGIC.

FAIR ENOUGH.

C'MON, WALT. KILL IT ALREADY.

YOU'VE GOT THIS!

WALT!

LOOK OUT!

THAT WAS COOL! WHAT AMULET WAS THAT?

RUU-UUUMBLE

The floor shook. I thought maybe Walt's magic was spreading into the building, which couldn't have been good.

-PLINK-

Walt didn't know.

Right about then, it sucked to be the serpent.

Felix's shoe bounced off another.

Julian's sword sliced off one of its heads.

A blast from Walt turned the third to dust.

Then Alyssa summoned a ton of stone to bury the monster.

CRUNCH!

CARTER, THAT WAS PART OF THE LESSON, RIGHT?

TELL ME THAT WAS PART OF THE LESSON.

YES... JUST A TEST.

I looked at Walt, and we came to a silent agreement: we needed to talk about this later.

But first, I had some questions of my own to answer.

CLASS DISMISSED.

**CLEOPATRA'S NEEDLE, LONDON.**

*My portal to London dropped me at Cleopatra's Needle.*

*After a brisk walk I stood in front of my grandparents' flat. It seemed so odd to be...home? I couldn't really call it that anymore.*

*Nervously, I knocked on the door. No answer.*

KNOCK KNOCK

*I was sure they were expecting me. I knocked again.*

GRAN?

GRAMPS?

CREEEEEAK...

*The living room was dark and empty. Gramps's television flickered with static, which wasn't right.*

*Gramps always kept the rugby matches on, even if he wasn't watching.*

SLAM

*My mind was just beginning to process a thought--**I am in danger**--when the front door slammed shut behind me.*

*If I had any blood of the pharaohs, it was turning to ice.*

Sniff
Whiff

*The smell of rotting meat wafted from upstairs.*

WELCOME HOME, SADIE KANE.

I'VE BEEN WAITING FOR YOU...

...FORTUNATELY, I'M VERY PATIENT.

WHO ARE YOU? WHERE ARE MY GRANDPARENTS?

DON'T YOU RECOGNIZE ME?

SADIE?

GRAN?!

NO! GET OUT OF MY GRAN!

I'D RATHER NOT.

YOUR FAMILY IS BLOOD OF THE PHARAOHS, AFTER ALL-- PERFECT HOSTS FOR A GODDESS LIKE ME.

DON'T MAKE ME STRAIN MYSELF, THOUGH.

YOUR GRANDMOTHER'S HEART ISN'T WHAT IT USED TO BE.

A goddess with black feathers who smells like death and who waits for something to die so she can eat it?

I KNOW YOU.

YOU'RE THE VULTURE GODDESS. NECKBUTT, IS IT?

IT'S NEKHBET!

I'VE COME TO OVERSEE YOUR DEATH. WE GODS DISAPPROVE OF YOUR PLAN TO WAKE RA AS LEADER OF THE BATTLE AGAINST APOPHIS.

My morning lesson had been crashed by a three-headed snake demon, but there was one huge takeaway from it.

Zia Rashid.

A few months ago, I'd fallen for a girl by the same name, who turned out to be a **shabti replica** of the real Zia.

Falling in love for the first time had been hard enough. But when the girl you like turns out to be ceramic and cracks to pieces before your eyes-- well, it gives "breaking your heart" a new meaning.

I had to rescue the real Zia.

All I knew was that her old mentor, Iskandar, had put her into a magical sleep and hidden her somewhere to keep her safe.

But I had no idea where the real Zia was--until now.

I consulted my scrying bowl.

It could show me anything I could visualize that wasn't disguised by magic. But places I'd never been to were hard to see. Still, I had to try.

"She sleeps in the place of red sands," the demon had said.

I passed my hand over the saucer and imagined the place of red sands.

Nothing happened.

The oil showed me only my own reflection.

KNOCK KNOCK.

HOW'S THE BOWL WORKING FOR YOU?

HI, WALT. IT'S WORKING FINE. HOW ARE YOU FEELING?

WHAT DO YOU MEAN?

THE TRAINING ROOM INCIDENT. THE THREE HEADED SNAKE. WHAT DID YOU THINK I MEANT?

OH, HEH-HEH. I GUESS IT NOW KNOWS OUR ABILITIES.

IT LEARNED FELIX THROWS A MEAN SHOE.

YEAH--

--BUT YOUR ABILITIES WERE THE STANDOUT!

THAT GRAY LIGHT YOU BLASTED THE SNAKE WITH.

AND THE WAY YOU HANDLED THE SHABTI PRACTICE DUMMY, TURNING IT TO DUST...?

YOU'RE WONDERING HOW I DID IT? HONEST, CARTER, IT WAS AN ACCIDENT. I PREFER USING AMULETS TO MAGIC IT'S *HEALTHIER* FOR ME.

*HEALTHIER* FOR YOU?

...

SOMETIMES I WONDER WHY I CAME HERE, THE TIMING...IT'S LIKE A BAD JOKE.

THINGS ARE COMPLICATED FOR ME, CARTER. AND THE FUTURE... I DON'T KNOW.

YOU'RE ONE OF OUR BEST!

IF IT'S SOMETHING ABOUT THE WAY SADIE AND I ARE *TEACHING*--

OF COURSE NOT. YOU'VE BEEN GREAT. AND SADIE--

SHE LIKES YOU A LOT. I KNOW SHE CAN COME ON A LITTLE STRONG. IF YOU WANT HER TO BACK OFF...

NO, IT'S NOTHING ABOUT SADIE!

I LIKE HER, TOO. I'M JUST--

At the mention of Sadie's name, the scrying oil began to change and stir.

WHA...?

The surface of the scrying oil erupted in flames.

SADIE'S IN TROUBLE!

WE HAVE TO GET TO LONDON!

DO YOU HAVE ANY TRANSPORTATION AMULETS?

WAY AHEAD OF YOU.

WE'LL RIDE THE JET STREAM AS GUSTS OF WIND!

THANKS TO MY TRUSTY *SHU** AMULET.

*God of the Winds.

SWISHH

With hindsight, I can now appreciate just what a miserable birthday I was having, but at the time I was too panicked to feel properly sorry for myself.

I raced around the corner of South Colonnade...

...and plowed straight into my best mates, *Liz and Emma.*

AHH! SADIE! WHAT'S WRONG?

NICE TO SEE YOU, TOO, WHERE ARE YOU RUSHING OFF--

I'LL EXPLAIN LATER!

UNLESS YOU'D LIKE TO BE RIPPED APART BY A GOD NAMED BOBBY, FOLLOW ME!

IS THIS ONE OF YOUR JOKES?

A GOD?

TWO GODS, ACTUALLY! THEY'VE TAKEN OVER MY GRAN AND GRAMPS. THEY WANT TO KILL ME.

NOW, UNLESS THERE ARE ANY MORE QUESTIONS-- RUN!

BUT I'M WEARING HEELS!

LOSE THEM!

*Anubis.*

*Much better looking than a jackal, eh?*

WHO-- AH--?

*Liz and Emma are not known for being smooth around good-looking boys. In fact, their brains more or less cease to function.*

UM, WAIT BY THE GATE? I'LL BE RIGHT BACK.

PLEASURE TO SEE YOU AGAIN, SADIE.

ER... NICE TO SEE YOU, TOO.

*Nice to see him? Not so much. He'd pretty much disappeared since last time I saw him.*

ARE YOU RUNNING TO ST. PETERSBURG? THE SECOND SECTION OF THE BOOK OF RA IS SITTING THERE.

BUT BE MINDFUL, IT'S A TRAP. MENSHIKOV IS HOPING TO BAIT YOU.

YEAH, NO--

I'VE GOT BIGGER PROBLEMS THAN THE BOOK OF RA AT THE MOMENT. TWO GODS HAVE POSSESSED MY GRANDPARENTS. IF YOU WANT TO LEND A HAND--

SADIE, I CAN'T INTERVENE.

I TOLD YOU WHEN WE FIRST MET, THIS ISN'T AN ACTUAL PHYSICAL BODY.

I CAN MANIFEST IN PLACES OF DEATH, LIKE THIS GRAVEYARD, BUT THERE IS VERY LITTLE I CAN DO OUTSIDE OF THEM HERE IN THE MORTAL REALM.

HOWEVER--

TAKE THIS. IT WILL HELP.

NOT AGAINST NEKHBET OR BABI, BUT IN YOUR GREATER QUEST TO AWAKEN RA.

IT'S A NETJERI BLADE, MADE FROM METEORIC IRON. IT'S USED FOR A CEREMONY CALLED *THE OPENING OF THE MOUTH.*

YES, WELL, IF I SURVIVE THE DAY, I'LL BE SURE TO TAKE THIS RAZOR AND OPEN SOMEONE'S MOUTH. THANKS EVER SO MUCH.

WELL, THEN, GOD OF PRETTY MUCH NOTHING USEFUL, ANYTHING ELSE BEFORE I GET MYSELF KILLED?

TAKE *THE UNDERGROUND.* THERE'S A STATION HALF A BLOCK SOUTH. THEY WON'T BE ABLE TO TRACK YOU VERY WELL BELOW THE EARTH.

OH, AND I TOLD YOUR *DRIVER* TO COME GET YOU AT WATERLOO STATION.

MY DRIVER?

BAST COULDN'T JOIN YOU ON YOUR QUEST TO FIND THE BOOK OF RA, SO SHE CALLED ON A FRIEND TO CHAPERONE YOU.

I'M SORRY I CAN'T DO MORE. NOW, GO!

AND *HAPPY BIRTHDAY*, SADIE.

I should've been very cross with Anubis. Kissing me without permission--the nerve! But I stood there, paralyzed.

As he melted into mist and disappeared, the graveyard became normal again-- part of the regular, unshimmery world.

THERE THEY GO! KILL THEM!

SADIE, COME ON!

TO WATERLOO STATION!!

We bolted for the Canary Wharf tube station, my lips still tingling from my first kiss.

And if I was humming "Happy Birthday" and smiling stupidly as I fled for my life--well, that was nobody's business, was it?

On the train, I gave my mates the shortest recap possible--how I'd discovered my ancestry as a magician and left London. I told them about the rise of Apophis, and our insane idea to awaken the god Ra.

SADIE, WE BELIEVE YOU! I'VE NEVER HEARD YOU TALK SO SERIOUSLY ABOUT ANYTHING.

YOU--YOU'VE CHANGED.

IT'S MORE THAN THAT.

YOU SEEM OLDER. MORE MATURE.

Their voices were tinged with sadness and I realized my mates and I were growing apart.

Babi and Nekhbet caught up with us at Waterloo Station.

LET'S GET OUT OF HERE!

KILL THE KANE, BABI!

Outside in the cab stand, a strange little man held a placard with my name on it.

Was that the driver Anubis had mentioned?

ABOUT TIME! SADIE KANE? I'M BAST'S FRIEND. CALLED IN TO HELP YOU OUT!

SADIE KANE

Our driver released a magic blast of pure ugly so stron
it tore the essences off my grandparent

BOO!

OH, DEAR!

HA-HA!

FEW CAN WITHSTAND A FULL-FRONTAL *BOO!*

I could see *why*. He was still uglier than anyone else on the planet.

YEP, I CAN SCARE AWAY ALMOST ANYTHING--SPIRITS, DEMONS, EVEN OTHER GODS--

WHICH IS WHY THE EGYPTIAN COMMONERS LOVED ME.

GRAN, ARE YOU OKAY?

VULTURES... MEATPIES...

Suddenly, a huge wind picked up.

SWISHH

I couldn't believe our chauffeur was **Bes.**

I used to laugh about his pictures in museums--his bulging eyes, wagging tongue, and general lack of clothing.

We traded stories on the ride through London. After hearing what Sadie had been through, I didn't feel so bad about my day.

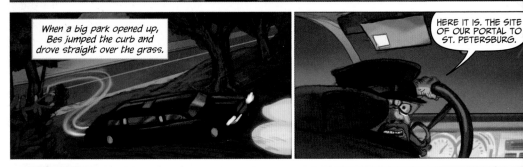

When a big park opened up, Bes jumped the curb and drove straight over the grass.

HERE IT IS. THE SITE OF OUR PORTAL TO ST. PETERSBURG.

THESE SPHINXES WERE BUILT FOR THE GRAND EXHIBITION OF BRITISH IMPERIAL MIGHT BACK IN 1851.

ALL GREAT EMPIRES WANT A PIECE OF EGYPT.

THIS IS WHERE YOU GET OUT, RIGHT, WALT?

WHY CAN'T WALT COME WITH US?

IT'S NOTHING REALLY. IT'S JUST... I SHOULD HELP OUT AT BROOKLYN HOUSE.

IT'S NOT THAT I *WANT* TO GO BACK--

--BUT YOU CAN'T GO WITH US. GO ON, KID. IT'S FINE.

SADIE, ABOUT YOUR BIRTHDAY...

HERE'S SOMETHING I MADE FOR YOU.

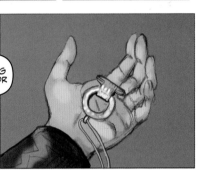

IT'S CALLED *SHEN!* THE SYMBOL THAT SURROUNDS RA'S SUN CROWN, A NEVER-ENDING LOOP, THE SYMBOL OF ETERNITY!

ETERNITY?!

YEAH, UM, I THOUGHT SINCE YOU'RE TRYING TO FIND RA, MAYBE IT'LL BRING YOU LUCK.

I MEANT TO GIVE IT TO YOU THIS MORNING, BUT... I KIND OF LOST MY NERVE.

WALT, I DON'T-- I MEAN, THANK YOU, BUT--

HAPPY BIRTHDAY, SADIE.

AND REMEMBER, IF YOU EVER NEED ME, YOUR AMULET'S LINKED TO MINE.

VROOOMM

WE'VE GOT WORK TO DO!

ST. PETERSBURG, RUSSIA. MARCH 18TH, MIDNIGHT.

*The other end of the portal was snowier but just as sphinx-y.*

FARTHEST-NORTH EGYPTIAN ARTIFACTS IN THE WORLD!

PILLAGED AND BROUGHT UP HERE TO DECORATE RUSSIA'S IMPERIAL CITY, ST. PETERSBURG. LIKE I SAID, EVERY NEW EMPIRE WANTS A PIECE OF EGYPT.

ACROSS THE RIVER, YOU CAN SEE MENSHIKOV'S STRONGHOLD-- THE *HERMITAGE MUSEUM.*

I WON'T BE ABLE TO GO WITH YOU--MY GODLY PRESENCE WILL SET OFF ALL SORTS OF ALARMS.

ALSO, YOU WON'T BE ABL TO SNEAK VER FAR SHIVERING LIKE THAT.

SNAP!

THANKS, BES!

NOW, I DON'T KNOW WHAT AMOS TOLD YOU ABOUT MENSHIKOV--

--BUT IF IT IMPLIED ANYTHING OTHER THAN A *SADISTIC TORTURER*, AMOS WAS JUST BEING POLITE. IF YOU NEED TO FIND HIM, JUST LISTEN FOR THE BLOODCURDLING SCREAMS.

ALSO, IF YOU HAVE ANY *STEALTH MAGIC*, NOW'S THE TIME TO USE IT. GOOD LUCK! I'LL FIND YOU WHEN YOU'RE DONE.

*We ran into the night.*

*Soon enough, we were at the front door of the Hermitage.*

THIS LOOKS LIKE THE ENTRANCE. I DON'T KNOW ANY STEALTH MAGIC. HOW ABOUT YOU CARTER?

I DO! GET UNDER THIS BLANKET.

NOW I JUST SPEAK THE COMMAND WORD--

I'MUN!*

*"Hide!"*

INSTANT INVISIBILITY SHROUD!

WHEN DID YOU MASTER THE SPELL?

ACTUALLY I'M STILL--

I'M STILL WORKING ON IT.

NOW-- WHERE DO YOU THINK MENSHIKOV'S SPOT WOULD BE AROUND HERE?

MERCY!

Bloodcurdling scream—
To find Menshikov, jus
follow the screaming.

DON'T FUSS, DEATH-TO-CORKS, YOU KNOW I NEED A SACRIFICE TO SUMMON SUCH A *MAJOR GOD*. IT'S NOTHING PERSONAL.

Major god?

The House of Life
didn't allow mortals
to summon gods.
It was the main reaso
Desjardins hated us

Menshikov was
supposedly his best
bud. So what was
he doing, breaking
the rules?

ONLY THE MOST PAINFUL FORM OF BANISHMENT WILL GENERATE ENOUGH ENERGY.

HURTS! SERVED YOU FOR FIFTY YEARS, MASTER. PLEASE!

NOW, NOW, I HAVE TO USE EXECRATION.

YOU WILL TELL ME THE SPELL FOR APOPHIS'S BINDINGS, SO HIS MINIONS AND I MAY FREE HIM. THE SPRING EQUINOX IS ALMOST UPON US!

THE BINDING FOR APOPHIS? I WONDER WHAT YOUR MASTER DESJARDINS WOULD THINK IF HE FOUND OUT YOUR REAL PLAN, AND THE SORT OF FRIENDS YOU KEEP.

DESJARDINS IS NOT MY MASTER... THE SERPENT IS SUPREME! NOW, WILL YOU DO AS I ASK, OR SHALL I *COERCE* YOU?

OH, NO NEED FOR COERCION. I'LL COOPERATE!

LET'S SEE... WHAT DID RA USE FOR A BASE?

SCARABS, LOTS AND LOTS OF SCARABS.

ALSO, A SACRIFICIAL VICTIM WOULD BE GOOD!

MAYBE A YOUNG IDIOT MAGICIAN WHO CAN'T DO A PROPER INVISIBILITY SPELL, LIKE CARTER KANE OVER THERE!

EH?

FIZZLE

SET! I'LL KICK YOU IN THE BA FOR THAT!

KANES?!

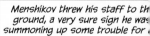

Menshikov threw his staff to th ground, a very sure sign he wa summoning up some trouble for

I'd really had enough snakes for one week.

SERPENTS ARE MY SPECIALTY!

AND THIS PARTICULAR CREATURE IS MY FAVORITE: *THE TJESU HERU.*

TWO HUNGRY MOUTHS TO FEED. TWO TROUBLESOME CHILDREN. PERFECT!

*HSSSS*

TOO BAD I'M STUCK IN THIS JAR, OR I MAY HAVE TO CHOOSE SIDES AND HELP SOMEONE!

SHUT UP, SET.

NO ONE IS CRAZY ENOUGH TO TRUST YOU.

CRAZY? I DON'T THINK SO.

DESPERATE? YES!

OKAY, SET. YOU'RE ON.

HA-DI!!!*

*"Destroy!!!"

CHOMP

This was the final insult. Possess my grandparents, attack my friends, ruin my birthday...

But don't ever hurt my brother.

Don't ask me how I did it. Though I will say my magic's stronger when I'm angry.

I didn't think. I simply channeled all my rage and shock into my staff.

I couldn't carry Carter by myself, but I had to get him out of there. We were in enemy territory. I needed to find Bes.

NEED A HAND?

LET'S GET YOUR BROTHER OUT OF HERE, SHALL WE? VLADIMIR IS NOT IN A GOOD MOOD.

Set volunteered to carry Carter, but I wasn't about to let the god of chaos take full charge of my brother, so we dragged him between us.

Set chatted amiably about tjesu heru poison:

COMPLETELY CURABLE! FATAL ABOUT TWELVE HOURS.

IT'S AMAZING STUFF!

And all the exciting ways the magicians might kill me once they caught up:

OH, YOU'RE TOAST, MY DEAR! A DOZEN SENIOR MAGICIANS WERE RALLYING TO MENSHIKOV WHEN I MADE MY, ER, STRATEGIC RETREAT!

And his tussle with Menshikov:

SIX VASES BROKEN OVER HIS HEAD, AND HE STILL SURVIVES!

I ENVY HIS THICK SKULL.

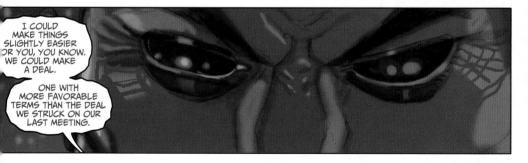

I COULD MAKE THINGS SLIGHTLY EASIER FOR YOU, YOU KNOW. WE COULD MAKE A DEAL.

ONE WITH MORE FAVORABLE TERMS THAN THE DEAL WE STRUCK ON OUR LAST MEETING.

Last time I talked to Set, I'd gained possession of his secret name, part of his soul. I used it as leverage to make him stay away from Carter and me and to stop making trouble around the world. It worked--but if there's one thing gods of chaos don't like, it's being controlled.

YOU WANT ME TO GIVE YOU BACK YOUR SECRET NAME.

BINGO.

A secret name wasn't just a name. It was the sum of the god's experiences. The more you understood the god, the closer you got to knowing their secret name, and the more you could channel their power.

IF YOU THINK I'D TRADE YOUR SECRET NAME TO GET A COUPLE OF LOUSY RUSSIAN MAGICIANS OFF MY TAIL, YOU'VE GOT ANOTHER THING COMING.

PERISH THE THOUGHT! I ONLY HOPE TO TELL YOU THE LOCATION OF THE FINAL SCROLL IN THE *BOOK OF RA*.

THAT *IS* WHAT YOU'RE AFTER ISN'T IT?

WHY WOULD YOU KNOW THAT?

COME NOW, SADIE. I WAS A LOYAL LIEUTENANT OF RA.

IF YOU WERE RA, AND YOU DIDN'T WANT TO BE BOTHERED BY ANY OLD MAGICIAN TRYING TO WAKE YOU...

...WOULDN'T YOU TRUST THE KEY TO YOUR LOCATION WITH YOUR MOST FEARSOME SERVANT?

GOOD POINT. OKAY, WHERE IS IT?

NOT SO FAST. MY SECRET NAME FIRST, THEN THE LOCATION.

IT'S QUITE SIMPLE. JUST SAY "I GIVE YOU BACK YOUR NAME." YOU'LL FORGET THE PROPER WAY TO SAY IT--

--AND THEN I'LL HAVE NO POWER OVER YOU! YOU'LL KILL ME!

YOU HAVE MY WORD THAT I WON'T.

YOU KILLED MY DAD!

ONLY SO HE COULD LIVE A MORE MEANINGFUL AFTERLIFE AS HOST TO OSIRIS.

YOU'RE OUT OF GOOD OPTIONS, SADIE KANE. MENSHIKOV WILL FIND A WAY INTO APOPHIS'S PRISON IN THE DUAT WITH OR WITHOUT HELP, AND MY BET IS HE'LL TRY ON THE EQUINOX, TWO DAYS FROM NOW.

WHEN CARTER DIES FROM THE TJESU HERU'S VENOM YOU'LL BE ALONE WITH NO CLUE WHERE TO FIND THE THIRD SCROLL.

*Another good point.*

ALL RIGHT, SET. BUT I'LL GIVE YOU ONE LAST ORDER.

YOU ARE NOT TO HARM THE KANE FAMILY.

YOU'LL MAINTAIN THE TRUCE WITH US AT LEAST UNTIL... UNTIL RA HAS BEEN AWAKENED.

OR UNTIL YOU TRY AND FAIL TO AWAKEN HIM?

IF THAT HAPPENS, THE WORLD'S OVER ANYWAY.

IN EXCHANGE FOR YOUR NAME, YOU WILL TELL ME THE LOCATION OF THE LAST PART OF THE BOOK OF RA, WITHOUT TRICKERY OR DECEPTION.

THEN YOU'LL DEPART FOR THE DUAT.

WE HAVE A DEAL. YOU'LL FIND THE SCROLL IN THE WASTELANDS OF THE EGYPTIAN DESERT, MY LAND, IN A PLACE CALLED *BAHARIYA.*

NOW, MY SECRET NAME, PLEASE.

I GIVE YOU BACK YOUR NAME.

*Just like that, I felt the magic leave me. I still knew Set's name: "Evil Day." But somehow I couldn't remember exactly how I used to say it, or how it worked in a spell. The memory had been erased.*

I HOPE YOU LIVE AFTER ALL, SADIE KANE. YOU'RE QUITE AMUSING.

AND JUST BECAUSE I LIKE YOU SO MUCH, I HAVE A FREE PIECE OF INFORMATION FOR YOUR BROTHER.

TELL HIM ZIA RASHID'S VILLAGE WAS CALLED *AL-HAMRAH MAKAN.*

WHY IS THAT--

HAPPY TRAVELS!

GOSH, THANKS.

NOW WHERE--HUFF-- IS BES?

THERE YOU ARE! I SAW A FLASH AND WENT SEARCHING FOR YOU.

WHAT'S UP WITH CARTER?

VROOOMM

POISONED. TJESU HERU ATTACK.

LET'S GET HIM OUT OF HERE. QUICK!

WE'RE BEING TAILED.

A block away, two white sports cars barreled toward us. A magician stuck his head out the sunroof of the lead car and pointed his staff in our direction.

WE HAVE THE SECOND SCROLL, AND I LEARNED THE LOCATION OF THE THIRD IS IN A PLACED CALLED BAHARIYA.

BAHARIYA!?

HOPE YOU CAN SWIM, KID.

THE CLOSEST PORTAL TO BAHARIYA IS ALEXANDRIA, WHICH IS A TRICKY PLACE TO TELEPORT TO.

IT'S CLEOPATRA'S OLD CAPITAL, WHERE THE EGYPTIAN EMPIRE FELL APART, SO MAGIC TENDS TO GET TWISTED AROUND.

THE ONLY WORKING PORTALS ARE IN THE OLD CITY, WHICH IS OFF THE COAST, UNDER THIRTY FEET OF WATER.

THIRTY FEET UNDERWATER!?

THERE'S AN EGYPTIAN BRIDGE OVER THE FONTANKA RIVER. WE'LL ACCESS THE ALEXANDRIA PORTAL THERE.

Why was there an Egyptian bridge built over the Fontanka River? No idea. Don't care--the only thing that mattered to me was that it could summon a portal.
W'PEH!*
ЕГИПЕТСКИИ МОСТ
*"Open!"
HOLD YOUR BREATH!
NEXT STOP: THE MEDITERRANEAN SEA!
On the other side, I had time to think: A teenager for less than a day, and I'm going to drown.
I blacked out.
But my **ba** did otherwise.

CHAPTER 4

HHMPH. YOU *SURVIVED.* NOW, HEAL ME.

*Isis spoke a spell and the venom retreated from Ra's veins. The swelling subsided and the two fang marks closed.*

*Ra's eyes faded from molten to mortal.*

AT LAST. NO PAIN. THE EXCHANGE IS COMPLETE. NOW, I SHALL RETIRE FROM THIS PLANE.

BUT MARK MY WORDS, ISIS-- I WILL NOT RETURN WHEN YOUR WEAK HUSBAND IS USURPED!

THE BALANCE BETWEEN MA'AT AND CHAOS WILL SLOWLY DEGRADE. EGYPT *ITSELF* WILL FALL.

THE NAMES OF HER GODS WILL FADE TO A DISTANT MEMORY.

WHEN THAT DAY COMES, REMEMBER HOW YOUR GREED AND AMBITION CAUSED IT TO HAPPEN.

THEN, ONE DAY, THE ENTIRE WORLD WILL STAND ON THE BRINK OF DESTRUCTION.

YOU WILL CRY OUT TO RA, AND I WILL NOT BE THERE.

*With the benefit of hindsight, I could see Ra's words would come to pass.*

*Osiris would be murdered by his brother, Set. **And though Isis's son Horus would one day retake the throne**, someday, Ra's other predictions would come true as well.*

ALEXANDRIA, EGYPT.
MARCH 18TH, NOON.

GASP--

I WAS BEGINNING TO THINK YOU'D NEVER WAKE UP.

SORRY FOR THE ROUGH ARRIVAL, BUT I PULLED YOU BOTH OUT OF THE MEDITERRANEAN AND GOT YOU TO THE HOTEL, DIDN'T I?

WE'RE IN ALEXANDRIA?

YEP, FOUR SEASONS HOTEL, PENTHOUSE SUITE! I CALLED IN SOME FAVORS TO GET US HERE.

IT'S ABOUT NOON. IT'S BEEN ALMOST TWELVE HOURS SINCE HE GOT BIT.

YOU'RE JUST IN TIME TO PAY YOUR FINAL RESPECTS TO CARTER.

NO!! I THINK I JUST SAW A WAY TO HELP HIM.

I reached in my bag for the Carter figurine Jaz had given me.

"You'll need this soon," she'd said.

CARTER, I CAN HEAL YOU. BUT I NEED YOUR HELP.

I NEED YOUR *SECRET NAME*.

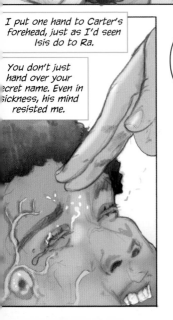

I put one hand to Carter's forehead, just as I'd seen Isis do to Ra.

You don't just hand over your secret name. Even in sickness, his mind resisted me.

YOU CAN DO THIS, BROTHER. I LOVE YOU. ALL THE EMBARRASSING BITS, ALL THE ANNOYING BITS--A THOUSAND ZIAS MIGHT RUN AWAY FROM YOU IF THEY KNEW THE TRUTH.

BUT I WON'T.

I'LL STILL BE HERE. NOW, TELL ME YOUR NAME, YOU BIG IDIOT, SO I CAN SAVE YOUR LIFE.

With his last bit of willpower, he told me his name. (Of course, I won't tell you what it is!)

*Now that I'd been in his mind, I knew he'd never rest until he'd found Zia. It went far beyond liking the girl. She was part of his destiny.*

I HAVE TO SAVE HER.

CAN'T. WE'RE PRESSED FOR *TIME*, KIDS.

THERE'S NOT ENOUGH OF IT TO DO A *SIDE MISSION*.

WE'LL HAVE TO SEPARATE. BES, YOU TAKE CARTER TO GO AFTER ZIA.

I'LL TRACK DOWN THE SCROLL.

SADIE, I PROMISED BAST I'D WATCH OVER YOU AND KEEP YOU SAFE.

I CAN'T LET YOU GO ALONE INTO THE DESERT.

*I unclasped my shen necklace.*

I WON'T GO ALONE. *WALT* OFFERED TO HELP.

BUT--

WALT CAN'T GO!

BUT YOU WON'T TELL ME WHY. WHATEVER HIS BLOODY SECRET IS, IT'S DRIVING HIM MISERABLE.

HE WANTS TO HELP, AND I'M GOING TO LET HIM.

*Our shen amulets were connected.*

*With a bit of effort, I was able to literally pull him through the Duat to my side.*

*Quite a handy magic item--instant hot guy.*

!?

HI, WALT. WE'RE GOING ON A MISSION TOGETHER.

HOW WILL WE FIND EACH OTHER?

WE'LL MEET BACK HERE. IT SHOULDN'T TAKE LONGER THAN TWENTY-FOUR HOURS FOR ME TO FIND THE SCROLL, YOU TO FIND ZIA'S VILLAGE, AND BOTH OF US TO GET BACK TO ALEXANDRIA.

ALEXANDRIA

Israel

Egypt

CAIRO

BAHARIYA ✗

✗
AL HAMRAH MAKAN

*Carter looked at me hopefully, but I think I knew even then that we wouldn't meet in Alexandria.*

*We were the Kanes, which meant everything would go wrong.*

IF YOU FREE HER, SHE COULD TURN TO WATER--OR DROWN!

WE CAN'T LEAVE HER LIKE THIS.

As I approached Zia's sarcophagus, the water began to shimmer. A current rippled down the sides, tracing the same symbol over and over, the symbol for Nephthys.

In her hands, she held a *crook and flail*, symbols for the pharaoh.

...or three months, I'd dreamed of finding Zia. Now I was almost too scared to wake her. What if she woke up and decided that she hated me?

I wanted to believe she possessed shared memories with her shabti, so that she would remember the times we'd had together. But if she hadn't, I wasn't sure I could stand the rejection.

I touched her tomb...

...and broke the spell!

Zia couldn't breathe.

NOW YOU DID IT, KID!

HER BODY IS REJECTING THE SPIRIT OF NEPHTHYS.

GET HER UPSTAIRS! TO THE RIVER!

HKK-- HKK

I AM SORRY FOR USING HER AS A HOST. IT WAS A POOR CHOICE, WHICH ALMOST DESTROYED US BOTH. GUARD HER WELL, CARTER KANE.

I SHALL RETURN TO MY PROPER BODY... THE NILE RIVER.

Zia still couldn't breathe.

I did the only thing I could think of.

HKK HKK

I tried mouth-to-mouth resuscitation.

SMACK!

DON'T YOU *DARE* KISS ME!

COME WITH US, PLEASE. I'M YOUR FRIEND. WE CAN PROTECT YOU.

NO ONE PROTECTS ME!

I AM A SCRIBE IN THE HOUSE OF LIFE!

BAHARIYA, EGYPT.
MARCH 18TH, TWO HOURS EARLIER.

*While Carter and Bes were busy being destroyed, Walt and I found Bahariya Oasis on a couple of magic camels, summoned by one of Walt's amulets.*

THE SCROLLS ARE GETTING HOT. I THINK WE'RE HERE.

WHY THE LONG FACE, WALT?

SORRY. I WAS... *THINKING.*

YOU KNOW, SOMETIMES *TALKING* HELPS.

IT'S HARD FOR ME TO TALK ABOUT IT.

I DIDN'T MEAN TO HIDE ANYTHING FROM YOU.

WELL, IT'S NOT TOO LATE.

LET'S GET THIS SCROLL.

IT SHOULD BE SOMEWHERE UNDERGROUND. I'M GUESSING.

THOSE MUMMIES LOOK DIFFERENT...

THEY SHOULD! BAHARIYA WAS A *GRECO-ROMAN* BURIAL GROUND. THEY ADOPTED THEIR OWN STYLE OF MUMMIES, DIFFERENT FROM THOSE IN EGYPTIAN SITES.

In the next chamber, we found nothing except a red lacquered box on a sandstone pedestal. On top of the box was a carved wooden handle shaped like a demonic greyhound with tall ears--the **Set animal**.

I walked straight up to the box, opened the lip, and grabbed the scroll inside.

EASY!

WALT!? WHAT'S WRONG?

NOTHING...

IT DOESN'T LOOK LIKE NOTHING.

WHATEVER YOUR SECRET IS, YOU CAN'T KEEP HIDING IT!

I'M CURSED, SADIE.

NOT JUST ME, MY ENTIRE ROYAL LINE. IT'S BEEN THAT WAY SINCE MY ANCESTOR *AKHENATEN*.

HE WAS THE PHARAOH WHO DECIDED TO DO AWAY WITH ALL THE OLD GODS AND JUST WORSHIP ATEN, THE SUN.

NOT THE SUN GOD RA-- THE ACTUAL SUN DISK, ATEN. THIS WAS UNTHINKABLE TO THE MAGICIANS OF THE TIME, ESPECIALLY THE PRIESTS OF AMUN-RA--

--SAME AS MENSHIKOV IS DESCENDED FROM--

YEAH! WELL, THEY CURSED AKENATEN AND HIS BLOODLINE.

AKENATEN'S SON *TUTANKHAMEN* WAS THE FIRST TO DIE OF THE CURSE.

YOU'RE RELATED TO *KING TUT*?

THE CURSE PROGRESSES IN ME NO MATTER WHAT I DO. SOME DAYS IT'S NOT SO BAD. SOME DAYS MY WHOLE BODY IS IN PAIN. WHEN I DO MAGIC, IT GETS WORSE.

THAT'S HOW I GOT INTO TALISMANS AND AMULETS. THEY STORE THEIR OWN MAGIC, AND DON'T REQUIRE AS MUCH FROM THE USER.

SO THE MORE MAGIC YOU DO...

...THE FASTER I DIE.

YOU IDIOT! WHY ARE YOU HERE, THEN?

YOU SHOULD'VE TOLD ME TO SHOVE OFF!

BES WARNED YOU TO STAY IN BROOKLYN. WHY DIDN'T YOU LISTEN?

ISN'T IT OBVIOUS?

*When Walt looked at me in that dusty tomb, his eyes were every bit as dark, tender, and sad as Anubis's.*

I'M GOING TO DIE ANYWAY, SADIE.

I WANT MY LIFE TO MEAN SOMETHING. AND... I WANT TO SPEND AS MUCH TIME AS I CAN WITH YOU.

I AM KNOWN AS A CREATION GOD AND AS THE OPENER OF DOORS. AND THERE'S A VERY IMPORTANT DOOR THAT YOU NEED.

YOUR BROTHER IS IN A GREAT DEAL OF TROUBLE.

CAN YOU SEND US THERE?

THOUGHT YOU'D NEVER ASK.

WHAT WILL WE FACE ON THE OTHER SIDE?

ENEMIES AND FRIENDS, BUT WHICH ARE WHICH, I CAN'T SAY. IF YOU SURVIVE, GO TO THE TOP OF THE *GREAT PYRAMID*. THAT SHOULD DO NICELY FOR AN ENTRY POINT INTO THE DUAT.

YOU'LL NEED TO FOLLOW RA'S JOURNEY ALONG THE RIVER OF NIGHT TO--

--CHOKE--

LOSING CONTROL OF HOST--

!!

I'll admit I needed help. Bes was locked in a glowing fluorescent cage. Zia was convinced we were enemies. My sword and wand were gone. I was holding a stolen crook and flail. And two of the most powerful magicians in the world were ready to arrest me, try me, and execute me.

Just then, Sadie and Walt tumbled upon Bes's cage, and the bars broke into splinters of light.

HOW--

Menshikov's and Dejardins's expressions turned to astonishment, and they disintegrated on the spot.

YOU KILLED THEM!

NAH. JUST SCARED 'EM BACK HOME.

THEY MAY BE UNCONSCIOUS FOR A FEW HOURS WHILE THEIR BRAINS TRY TO PROCESS MY *MAGNIFICENT PHYSIQUE*, BUT THEY'LL LIVE. MORE IMPORTANT--

YOU TWO HAD THE NERVE TO ANCHOR A PORTAL ON ME? DO I *LOOK* LIKE A *RELIC*?

IT WASN'T OUR IDEA! *PTAH* SENT US HERE TO HELP YOU...

AFTER WE GOT THE THIRD SCROLL!

NICE WORK, SADIE!

IS THAT... ARE YOU THE REAL ZIA?

GET AWAY!

WE'RE NOT GOING TO HURT YOU!

Zia's legs shook.

Her hands trembled.

Then she did the only logical thing for someone who'd been through what she had after a three-month coma.

STRONG GIRL. SHE HELD UP UNDER A FULL-FRONTAL BOO! STILL... WE'D BETTER PICK HER UP AND GET OUT OF HERE.

DESJARDINS WON'T STAY GONE FOREVER.

LET'S MAKE HASTE, THEN! PTAH SAYS THE ENTRYWAY TO THE DUAT WE'LL NEED IS IN THE GREAT PYRAMID IN CAIRO.

PLEASE TELL ME YOU HAVE A CAR.

BETTER.

NOT ONLY DO WE HAVE A CAR, WE HAVE BEDOUINS!

KWAI, ISN'T IT?

AS I RECALL, YOU WERE EXILED TO THE THREE-HUNDREDTH NOME IN NORTH KOREA FOR MURDERING A FELLOW MAGICIAN.

AND YOU, *SARAH JACOBI!*

YOU WERE SENT TO ANTARCTICA FOR CAUSING THE TSUNAMI IN THE INDIAN OCEAN.

MANY OF THESE MAGICIANS HAVE HAD ISSUES IN THE PAST, BUT IF YOU WANT BROOKLYN HOUSE *DESTROYED*, WE MUST BE RUTHLESS.

AND YOU, VLADIMIR? WILL YOU LEAD THEM?

NO, MY LORD. I HAVE FULL CONFIDENCE THAT THIS, AH, FINE GROUP CAN DEAL WITH BROOKLYN ON THEIR OWN. THEY WILL ATTACK AT SUNSET TOMORROW.

AS FOR ME, I WILL ENTER THE *DUAT* AND DEAL WITH THE KANES *PERSONALLY.* IF THEY HAVE ALL THREE SCROLLS, THAT'S WHERE THEY'LL BE, TRYING TO WAKE RA BEFORE THE DAWN OF THE EQUINOX.

GO, GET THOSE CREATURES OUT OF MY SIGHT.

WE WILL SAVE THE HOUSE OF LIFE. THE KANES WILL BE DESTROYED, THE GODS PUT BACK INTO EXILE, I SWEAR IT.

YOU, MY LORD, SHOULD STAY *HERE AND REST.*

I WILL SEND A SCRYING BOWL TO YOUR QUARTERS SO YOU MAY OBSERVE OUR PROGRESS.

I WILL "OBSERVE" VLADIMIR.

BUT I WILL NOT *REST.*

Zia took some convincing, but after explaining all that Menshikov had been up to, and what she'd witnessed at al-Hamrah Makan, we persuaded her not to blast us with any more flames.

Bes told us the portal to the Duat could only be opened at sunset, so we killed time in our hotel room playing an ancient game called **Senet.**

THAT'S A THREE! *HA!*

BEAT THAT, GIRLS!

# CHAPTER 5

IT'S GETTING TO BE *SUNSET*. THAT'S WHAT WE'RE KILLING TIME FOR, RIGHT?

YEP. WE'RE CLOSE ENOUGH TO THE EQUINOX NOW THAT ALL THE PORTALS IN THE WORLD ARE SHUT DOWN EXCEPT FOR TWO TIMES: SUNSET AND SUNRISE, WHEN NIGHT AND DAY ARE PERFECTLY BALANCED.

IF YOU'RE GOING TO STOP APOPHIS'S RISE, WE HAVE TO GET YOU TO THE *DUAT*.

ONCE THERE, YOU'LL READ THE BOOK OF RA AT VARIOUS STAGES IN THE *TWELVE HOUSES OF NIGHT* TO TRY TO UNLOCK RA'S SOUL.

WAIT. IF THE MAGICIANS ARE GOING TO ATTACK BROOKLYN HOUSE, WON'T THEY HAVE TO GO AT SUNSET, TOO?

GET YOUR PRIORITIES STRAIGHT, KID.

YOU WANT TO DEFEND YOUR FRIENDS, OR SAVE THE WORLD FROM THE SERPENT?

I'LL GO TO BROOKLYN.

I HAVE SOME INFLUENCE WITH OTHER MAGICIANS-- AT LEAST I DID, BEFORE RED SANDS.

WHAT IF YOU HAVE TO FIGHT?

LET'S HOPE FOR THEIR SAKE IT DOESN'T COM TO THAT.

I'LL GO WITH YOU, ZIA.

IT'S SETTLED.

WE'LL GET TO THE PYRAMID AT SUNSET, WHERE I'LL OPEN TWO PORTALS-- ONE FOR WALT AND ZIA TO BROOKLYN, THE OTHER FOR YOU AND SADIE TO THE DUAT.

IT'LL BE DANGEROUS, RECKLESS. PROBABLY FATAL.

SO, AN AVERAGE DAY FOR US.

SADIE'S RIGHT.

YOU ARE... HOW DID SHE PUT IT? ENDEARINGLY CLUMSY.

THIS ONE'S FOR US.

COMING?

CARTER!

ADIOS, KIDS. I'LL FOLLOW YOU INTO THE DUAT, AS SOON AS I GET WALT AND ZIA THROUGH THEIR PORTAL.

I'LL MEET YOU ON THE RIVER OF NIGHT, IN *THE FOURTH HOUSE.*

YOU'LL SEE. NOW, GO!

The portal let us off on a boat I recognized from my **ba** trip to the Age of the Gods as Ra's. It was far more run-down than last time.

LOOKS LIKE WE'RE HERE?

Also, the Duat gave us an Egyptian makeover.

NICE SKIRT AND EYELINER, CARTER!

HUH? RA'S CROOK AND FLAIL--THEY'RE GLOWING!

A crew of fireballs shot from Ra's crook and flail.

The crew scattered to take up their stations.

The leaky hull groaned as the barque turned its nose downstream.

UM... ONWARD!

YOU ARE AT ITS GATES.

AND YOU WON'T MAKE IT PAST.

IF YOU KNEW MY NAME, WE WOULDN'T NEED INTRODUCTIONS, AND I COULD LET YOU PASS.

UNFORTUNATELY, NO ONE EVER KNOWS MY NAME.

I'M TERRIBLY SORRY I HAVE TO SLICE YOU TO PIECES.

HIS NAME?! THAT'S *KHNUM!*

CARTER, I DON'T THINK THAT NAME WILL WORK. HE WANTS US TO TELL HIS *SECRET* NAME.

*I opened the Book of Ra and began to read the first part of the spell.*

"I NAME YOU FIRST FROM CHAOS, KHNUM, WHO IS RA, THE EVENING SUN. I SUMMON YOUR *BA* TO AWAKEN THE GREAT ONE...

"...FOR I AM SADIE KANE, RESTORER OF THE THRONE OF FIRE!"

The nurses' desk was a crescent of granite in front of a stone disk with a triangular fin--a sundial, which seemed strange, as there was no sun.

Behind the counter, a heavy woman stood with her back to us, checking a whiteboard with names and medication times.

EXCUSE US!

MAY I HELP YOU?

UM, HIPPO--I MEAN, HULLO!

MY BROTHER AND I ARE LOOKING FOR...

I glanced at Carter and found he was **not** staring at the nurse's face.

CARTER! EYES TOWARD HER *EYES*.

WHAT? RIGHT. SORRY. UH, YOU'RE A GODDESS, *TAWARET*, RIGHT?

WHY, HOW NICE TO BE RECOGNIZED! YES, DEAR. I'M TAWARET.

YOU SAID YOU WERE LOOKING FOR A RELATIVE, PERHAPS?

THEY WANT TO WAKE RA.

When Bes spoke, a twinkle of recognition flashed across Tawaret's eyes.

IS THAT...!? WHY YES, BES, IT'S *YOU*!!

HEY, TAWARET.

HE'S DOING US A FAVOR.

OUR FRIEND BAST ASKED HIM TO LOOK AFTER US.

I *SEE*. A FAVOR FOR BAST.

PLEASE. LOOK, THE FATE OF THE WORLD IS AT STAKE! IT'S VERY IMPORTANT WE FIND RA. WE WANT TO AWAKEN HIM.

IF THAT'S THE CASE, CHILDREN, YOU'RE RUNNING OUT OF TIME.

*Tawaret pointed to the sundial. The needle was inching toward the number five.*

THIS PLACE IS THE FOURTH HOUSE OF NIGHT! HOW CAN THE SUNDIAL BE MOVING TOWARD FIVE?

WE SHOULD BE FROZEN AT THE FOURTH HOUR!

DOESN'T WORK THAT WAY, KID. TIME IN THE MORTAL WORLD DOESN'T STOP PASSING JUST BECAUSE YOU'RE IN THE FOURTH HOUSE.

THE GATES TO THE HOUSES ARE CONNECTED TO THEIR TIMES OF NIGHT. WHICH MEANS--

--WE CAN STAY IN THE FOURTH HOUSE FOR AS LONG AS WE LIKE, BUT ONCE THAT DIAL HITS FIVE, WE'LL BE STUCK IN THE FOURTH HOUSE UNTIL IT ROLLS TO THE FOUR THE NEXT DAY!

THEN WE'D BEST HURRY TO THE DORMITORIES TO FIND RA!

I'LL SHOW YOU THE WAY. FOLLOW ME!

We passed so many bedrooms I lost count. Most of the doors were closed, but a few were open, showing frail old gods in their beds, staring at the flickering blue light of televisions or simply lying in the dark crying. After twenty or thirty such rooms, I stopped looking. It was too depressing.

I held the **Book of Ra**, hoping it would get warmer as we approached the sun god, but no such luck. I began to feel frantic.

THIS ISN'T **WORKING**.

DO YOU THINK THE SCROLL COULD GUIDE US?

IT'S NOT HEATING UP OR LIGHTING UP IN ANY WAY.

MAYBE IF I START TO READ THE SECOND PART OF THE SPELL--

SADIE, BE CAREFUL!

IF IT'S THE WRONG TIME, IT COULD BACKFIRE!

YOU COULD HAVE YOUR EYES RUINED LIKE MENSHIKOV OR WORSE!

I KNOW. BUT WE DON'T HAVE TIME TO WANDER THE HALLS FOREVER, AND RA WILL ONLY APPEAR IF WE INVOKE HIM. WE HAVE TO PROVE OURSELVES BY TAKING THE RISK.

"I INVOKE THE NAME OF RA, THE SLEEPING KING, LORD OF THE NOONDAY SUN, WHO SITS UPON THE THRONE OF FIRE..."

Well, you get the idea. I described how Ra rose from the sea of Chaos. I recalled his light shining on the primordial land of Egypt, bringing life to the Nile Valley.

As I read, I felt warmer.

SADIE, YOU'RE SMOKING.

I stayed focused on the scroll. I described Ra's sun boat sailing across the sky.

I spoke of his kingly wisdom and the battles he'd won against Apophis.

IS IT JUST ME OR IS THE SMOKE SHOWING US THE WAY?

YOU'RE DOING WELL, SADIE. THIS HALLWAY LOOKS FAMILIAR.

The spell led me to a door.

"RA, THE SUN'S ZENITH..."

Carter pushed it open and we stepped inside. I kept reading, though I was quickly approaching the end of the spell.

In the sputtering light of my spell, I saw the oldest man in the world sleeping in bed.

"THE LIGHT OF RA RETURNS."

I moved to his bedside and kept reading. I described Ra awakening at dawn, sitting in his throne as his boat climbed the sky, the plants turning toward the warmth of the sun.

The old man didn't move. His mouth was pursed like his lips had been sewn together.

"I SING THE PRAISES OF THE SUN GOD."

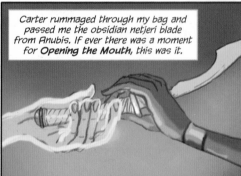

The god's mouth... of course.

I stretched out my free hand to Carter and snapped my fingers.

Carter rummaged through my bag and passed me the obsidian netjeri blade from Anubis. If ever there was a moment for **Opening the Mouth**, this was it.

I touched the knife to the old man's lips and spoke the last line of the spell.

"AWAKE, MY KING, WITH THE NEW DAY."

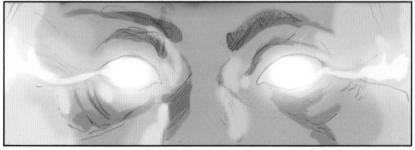

We boarded the sun boat. What was the point of continuing?
WEASEL COOKIES! ZEBRA!
CHAPTER 6

As soon as Ra stepped on the boat, brilliant light exploded around him, completely blinding me.

Ra stood with transformed clothes and before him, a chair of molten gold.

YOU... YOU SHOULD GO. PERHAPS OSIRIS CAN PROVIDE AN ANSWER.

Fun fact about the Kane family: our parents run the Duat. Been that way ever since our father decided to host Osiris, the lord of the underworld.

WHAT DO YOU THINK, SADIE?

MIGHT AS WELL...

SHALL WE VISIT MOM AND DAD?

We set sail for our father's island home on the Lake of Fire.

Our boat turned toward a dock, where a man and a woman stood waiting for us. Dad wore his usual brown suit. His skin glowed with a bluish tint. Mom shimmered in ghostly white.

SADIE, CARTER. IT'S GREAT TO SEE YOU!

WE'VE BEEN WATCHING YOUR PROGRESS.

YOU'VE BOTH BEEN SO BRAVE.

NOT THAT IT MATTERS MUCH.

THE BLOODY SUNDIAL-- THE STUPID GATES-- WE FAILED!

SHHH, NONE OF THAT. THIS IS A TIME TO REST AND RENEW.

I'M SO PROUD OF YOU BOTH.

COME, WE'VE PREPARED A FEAST.

The last time we'd visited our father, the place was dark and scary, fitting for a person who rules the Hall of Judgment.

But now it had a new life!

IT LOOKS DIFFERENT HERE!

YOUR MOTHER AND I HAVE BEEN SPLITTING OUR TIME BETWEEN HERE, FOR MY OSIRIS DUTIES, AND AARU, THE EGYPTIAN HEAVEN.

WE'VE GOT SOME INTERIOR DECORATING IDEAS FROM THERE.

PLEASE SIT.

*We ate. It tasted like perfection. But it was hard to enjoy.*

WE HAVEN'T FINISHED THE BOOK OF RA. WE NEED TO FIND KHEPRI.

YES, THE SCARAB GOD, RA'S FORM AS THE RISING SUN.

TO FIND HIM, YOU WOULD NEED TO PASS THROUGH THE GATES.

DAD, YOU DON'T HAVE A WAY THROUGH THE GATES, DO YOU?

CAN YOU TELEPORT US TO THE OTHER SIDE OR SOMETHING?

I WISH I COULD, BUT THE JOURNEY MUST BE FOLLOWED. IT IS PART OF RA'S REBIRTH.

YOU'RE RIGHT. YOU NEED EXTRA TIME.

THERE MIGHT BE A WAY, THOUGH I'D NEVER SUGGEST IT IF THE STAKES WEREN'T SO HIGH--

HIM?

YOU INVITED *HIM?*

WHO? WHAT DO YOU MEAN?

ME, I SUPPOSE.

MOON PIE.

KHONSU, THE MOON GOD, AT YOUR SERVICE. I'M SURE YOU'VE HEARD STORIES ABOUT ME.

I REMEMBER! YOU GAMBLED WITH NUT, AND SHE WON ENOUGH MOONLIGHT TO ADD FIVE EXTRA DAYS TO THE CALENDAR.

THAT LET HER GET AROUND RA'S COMMANDMENT THAT HER FIVE CHILDREN COULDN'T BE BORN ON ANY DAY OF THE YEAR.

BAD NUTS.

YES, NUT WAS A GAMBLER! AND I HAVE THE POWER TO CHANGE TIME.

THE MOON IS CHANGEABLE, YOU SEE. ITS LIGHT WAXES AND WANES. IN MY HANDS, TIME CAN ALSO WAX AND WANE. YOU NEED... WHAT, ABOUT THREE EXTRA HOURS?

I CAN WEAVE THAT FOR YOU OUT OF MOONLIGHT, IF YOU AND YOUR SISTER ARE WILLING TO *GAMBLE* FOR IT.

I CAN MAKE IT SO THAT THE GATES BEYOND THE FOURTH HOUSE HAVE NOT YET CLOSED.

SO WHAT DO YOU SAY, CARTER?

SADIE?

PLAY ME AT SENET.

FOR EACH PIECE I MOVE OFF THE BOARD, I'LL TAKE A *REN* FROM ONE OF YOU.

IT'S ONLY A PART OF YOUR SOUL. ROUGHLY ONE-FIFTH. NOT ENOUGH TO KILL YOU, JUST TURN YOU INTO A VEGETABLE, LIKE RA THERE.

NOW, WHO'S FEELING LUCKY?

CARTER AND SADIE, I BROUGHT KHONSU HERE SO THAT YOU'D HAVE THE CHOICE. WE DON'T EXPECT YOU TO TAKE THIS RISK.

BUT WHATEVER YOU DO, I'M STILL PROUD OF YOU BOTH.

IF THE WORLD ENDS TONIGHT, THAT WON'T CHANGE.

I UNDERSTAND, DAD. WE'RE KANES. WE DON'T RUN FROM HARD CHOICES.

CARTER'S RIGHT. KHONSU, WE'LL PLAY YOUR STUPID GAME.

EXCELLENT! THAT'S TWO SOULS. TWO HOURS TO WIN. AH, BUT YOU'LL NEED THREE HOURS TO GET THROUGH THE GATES ON TIME, WON'T YOU?

I'LL DO IT.

BES, YOU'VE DONE ENOUGH FOR US.

BAST WOULD NEVER EXPECT YOU--

I'M NOT DOING IT FOR BAST!

YOU KIDS ARE THE REAL DEAL.

FOR THE FIRST TIME IN AGES I'VE FELT *WANTED* AGAIN.

*IMPORTANT.* NOT LIKE A SIDESHOW ATTRACTION. IF THINGS GO WRONG, JUST TELL TAWARET...TELL HER I TRIED TO TURN BACK THE CLOCK.

WE CANNOT STAY FOR THIS. BUT, CHILDREN...

WE LOVE YOU. YOU WILL PREVAIL.

We played the game.

Khonsu wasn't too sympathetic to our mission to stop Apophis.

IF APOPHIS TAKES OVER AND SWALLOWS THE SUN, WELL, I SUPPOSE THE MOON WILL STILL BE THERE.

Khonsu tossed the sticks.

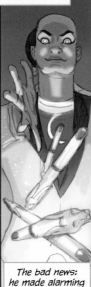

The bad news: he made alarming progress.

He rolled a five and got one of his pieces almost to the end of the board.

The good news: the piece got stuck at the House of Three Truths.

He could only roll a three to get it out.

CAREFUL NOW, THIS IS WHERE IT GETS INTERESTING.

Sadie rolled.

A *FOUR*. THAT GIVES US TWO OPTIONS. OUR LEAD PIECE COULD GO OUT.

OR OUR SECOND PIECE COULD BUMP KHONSU'S PIECE FROM THE HOUSE OF THREE TRUTHS AND SEND IT BACK TO THE START.

BUMP HIM. IT'S SAFER.

THEN WE'RE STUCK IN THE HOUSE OF THREE TRUTHS.

THE CHANCES OF KHONSU ROLLING A THREE ARE SLIM.

TAKE YOUR FIRST PIECE OUT.

THAT WAY YOU'LL BE ASSURED OF AT LEAST ONE EXTRA HOUR.

I moved our first piece four places, out of play.

CONGRATULATIONS! I OWE YOU ONE HOUR.

NOW IT'S MY TURN.

Khonsu's sticks clattered on the game board, and I felt like someone had snipped an elevator cable in my chest, plunging my heart straight down a shaft.

*Khonsu had rolled a **three**.*

OH, WHAT A SHAME. NOW, WHOSE SOUL DO I COLLECT FIRST?

NO, PLEASE! TRADE BACK. TAKE THE HOUR YOU OWE US INSTEAD.

THOSE AREN'T THE *RULES*.

TAKE MY REN, THE MOVE WAS MY IDEA.

BES, NO!

IT WAS PART OF THE STRATEGY, KIDS.

THE MOST IMPORTANT THING IS GETTING ALL THREE OF YOUR PIECES OFF THE BOARD, AND LOSING NO MORE THAN ONE.

THIS WAS THE ONLY WAY TO DO IT.

YOU'LL BEAT HIM EASILY NOW. SOMETIMES YOU HAVE TO LOSE A PIECE TO WIN A GAME.

BES, DON'T! THIS ISN'T RIGHT.

KID, YOU WERE WILLING TO SACRIFICE. ARE YOU SAYING I'M NOT AS BRAVE AS SOME PIPSQUEAK MAGICIAN?

NOW, WIN THE GAME AND GET OUT OF HERE.

AND WHEN YOU SEE MENSHIKOV...

KICK HIM IN THE KNEE FOR ME.

WHAT A DELIGHT! A GOD'S REN.

ARE YOU READY, BES?

I'M READY.

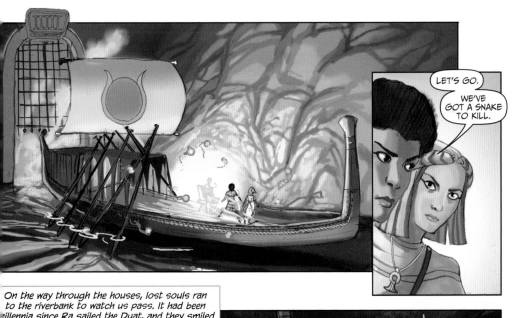

LET'S GO.

WE'VE GOT A SNAKE TO KILL.

On the way through the houses, lost souls ran to the riverbank to watch us pass. It had been millennia since Ra sailed the Duat, and they smiled as they basked in the sun god's warm light.

Next we passed through **Aaru**, the Egyptian version of paradise.

The **Eighth House**, the **House of Challenges**, wasn't very challenging. We fought monsters, yes. Serpents loomed out of the river. Demons arose. Ships full of ghosts tried to board the sun boat. We destroyed them all.

The **Ninth**, **Tenth**, and **Eleventh** houses passed in a blur. At last I heard a roar up ahead, like another waterfall or a stretch of rapids. We kept gaining speed.

We passed under a low archway carved like the goddess Nut. I got the feeling we were entering the **Twelfth House**, the last part of the Duat before we emerged into a new dawn.

THE PATH'S BEEN SABOTAGED.

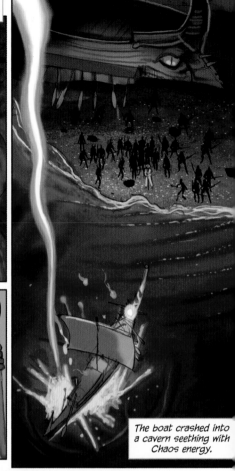

The boat crashed into a cavern seething with Chaos energy.

IT'S A TRAP. THE WORK OF APOPHIS!

I KNOW. LET'S GO TELL HIM WE DON'T LIKE HIS WORK.

WELCOME TO THE SERPENT'S PRISON!

GLAD YOU COULD JOIN US FOR THE END OF THE WORLD.

Carter and my kite had the demons covered.

And Menshikov was busy with the Chief Lector.

Time to read the last chapter in the Book of Ra.

"I INVOKE THE DAWN OF A NEW DAY.

"KHEPRI, THE SCARAB WHO RISES FROM DEATH, THE REBIRTH OF RA!"

The Book of Ra disappeared with a poof and the ground quaked.

KHEPRI!

HA HA HA!

I almost dared to hope we'd won.

WITH KHEPRI DISLODGED, THERE IS NOTHING TO HOLD THE REST OF THE SCARABS, OR APOPHIS, IN PLACE!

WELL DONE, SADIE KANE!

Chaos energy swept the scarabs off the beach, revealing red sand below.

Ahead of us, two doors materialized at the tunnel's end.

EACH NEW DAWN IS A NEW WORLD. MAYBE WE'LL BE HEALED.

RA, TOO?

Gates holding two giant golden scarab statues opened, and beyond them gleamed the morning skyline of Manhattan. The River of Night was emptying out into New York Harbor.

With daylight, I was starting to feel better, stronger, like I'd had a good night's sleep.

Our Chaos sickness disappeared as soon as we saw daylight.

WALT, ZIA! WHAT'S UP, GUYS?

THE ENEMY'S BEEN TRYING TO BREAK IN ALL NIGHT! AMOS AND BAST HAVE HELD THEM OFF, BUT--

ZEBRA!

IS THAT-- THAT ISN'T--

THIS IS--THIS IS RA, THE LORD OF THE SUN? WHY IS HE OFFERING ME A BUG?

I LIKE ZEBRAS.

WEASELS IS SICK?

Zebras...Zia. Weasels...Walt.

Before I could think about this further, Carter pulled me away!

COME ON, SADIE, WE HAVE TO SECURE THE VERANDA!

Our initiates knew the **hi-nehm*** spell well enough to fix most of the broken things.

*\* "bring together"*

And it's truly amazing how much polishing, dusting, and scrubbing one can accomplish by attaching large dusting cloths to the wings of a griffin.

By sunset, we had the mansion completely restored.

**?**

DID SOMEONE SUMMON A PORTAL?

I THINK THIS ONE'S FOR US, SADIE.

WELCOME, CARTER AND SADIE. WE ARE *HONORED.*

Horus's words didn't match his tone, which was stiff and formal.

On the other side, we found ourselves in the throne room of the gods, facing a crowd of assembled deities.

BEHOLD! CARTER AND SADIE KANE, WHO AWAKENED OUR KING!

LET THERE BE NO DOUBT: APOPHIS THE ENEMY HAS RISEN. WE MUST UNITE BEHIND RA.

WE WILL FIND A WAY TO DEFEAT APOPHIS! NOW, CELEBRATE THE RETURN OF RA! I EMBRACE CARTER KANE AS A BROTHER.

I PLEDGE MY LOYALTY! I EXPECT YOU ALL TO DO THE SAME. I WILL PROTECT RA'S BOAT AS WE PASS THROUGH THE DUAT TONIGHT.

EACH OF YOU SHALL TAKE TURNS WITH THIS DUTY UNTIL THE SUN GOD IS...FULLY RECOVERED.

He sounded absolutely unconvinced this would ever happen.

I HOPE YOU KNOW WHAT YOU'RE DOING, SADIE. OUR GREATEST ENEMY RISES, AND YOU HAVE DETHRONED MY SON AND MADE A SENILE GOD OUR LEADER.

GIVE IT A CHANCE ISIS.

HA! ANUBIS, SEE THESE TWO OUT.

GO NOW, CARTER. SEE WHAT YOUR VICTORY HAS COST.

LET US HOPE ALL YOUR ALLIES DO NOT SHARE SUCH A FATE.

WHAT DO YOU MEAN?

HE WANTED YOU TO SEE BES.

BES IS ALIVE?

BES IS IN TAWARET'S CARE. WITHOUT HIS REN, HE WILL REMAIN A HUSK.

I'M SORRY, SADIE. THE GODS CAN BE--

UNGRATEFUL? INFURIATING?

I couldn't help sobbing.

I remembered how we'd met at Waterloo Station, when he'd chauffeured Liz and Emma and me to safety. I remembered how he'd scared away Nekhbet and Babi in his ridiculous Speedo.

He had an enormous, colorful, ludicrous, wonderful personality-- and it seemed impossible that it was gone forever. He'd given his immortal life to buy us one extra hour.

WE CAN BE SLOW TO REALIZE WHAT IS IMPORTANT.

SOMETIMES, IT TAKES US A WHILE TO APPRECIATE SOMETHING NEW...

...SOMETHING THAT MIGHT CHANGE US FOR THE BETTER.

He fixed me with those warm eyes, and I wanted to melt into a puddle.

That evening I sat alone on my bed with the windows open. The first night of spring had turned surprisingly warm and pleasant. Lights glittered along the riverfront.

There was a knock at the door.

Had to be Carter coming to debrief.

COME IN!

HI, SADIE.

WALT?!

He blinked, obviously surprised by my lack of hospitality.

SORRY, I'LL GO.

NO! I MEAN... THAT'S ALL RIGHT. YOU JUST SURPRISED ME. AND--YOU KNOW...WE HAVE RULES ABOUT BOYS BEING IN THE GIRLS' ROOMS WITHOUT, UM, SUPERVISION.

WELL, YOU'RE THE INSTRUCTOR. CAN YOU SUPERVISE ME?

He leaned against the closet door. With some horror, I realized it was still open, revealing my picture of Anubis.

OH, YOU WANT ME TO CLOSE THIS?

YES. NO. POSSIBLY.

I MEAN, IT DOESN'T MATTER.

WELL, NOT THAT IT DOESN'T MATTER, BUT--

SADIE, I'M JUST HERE TO SAY...

THAT DAY IN THE DESERT, AT BAHARIYA...WOULD YOU THINK I'M CRAZY IF I TELL YOU THAT WAS THE BEST DAY OF MY LIFE?

WELL, EGYPTIAN DESERT, SMELLY CAMELS, POSSESSED DATE FARMERS...GOSH, IT WAS QUITE A DAY.

AND YOU.

YES, WELL, I SUPPOSE I BELONG IN THAT LIST OF CATASTROPHES.

SADIE, I JUST WANTED TO SAY, WHATEVER HAPPENS, I'M GLAD I MET YOU HERE IN BROOKLYN. AND WHATEVER HAPPENS WITH MY CURSE... IT'S OKAY.

IT'S NOT OKAY!

I'D HOPED YOU WOULD ALSO BE CURED BY RA'S RETURN AS JAZ WAS.

RA'S RETURN MAY NOT HAVE CURED ME, BUT IT STILL GAVE ME NEW HOPE. YOU'RE AMAZING, SADIE. ONE WAY OR ANOTHER, WE'RE GOING TO MAKE THIS WORK. I'M NOT LEAVING YOU.

HOW CAN YOU PROMISE THAT?

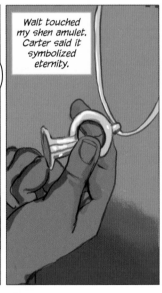

Walt touched my shen amulet. Carter said it symbolized eternity.

I thought he might kiss me, but something made us both hesitate--a sense that it would only make things more uncertain. More fragile.

JUST TRY NOT TO WORRY ABOUT ME.

Leave it to me to be completely torn between two amazing guys-- one who's dying and another who's the god of death. What sort of choice is that, I ask you?

A few moments after Walt left, Carter came in.

HEY, SIS!

IN ALL THE QUESTING, I FORGOT TO GIVE YOU A BIRTHDAY PRESENT.

IT'S, UM, NOT A GOLD NECKLACE. OR EVEN A MAGICAL KNIFE.

BUT I TOLD YOU I HAD A BIRTHDAY PRESENT FOR YOU. THIS-- THIS IS IT.

On the inside cover, a name was written in lovely cursive.

THIS BOOK
BELONGS TO
Ruby Kane

Blackley's Survey of the Sciences for First-Year College

twelfth edition

IT'S AN AMAZING BIRTHDAY PRESENT. AND YOU'RE AN AMAZING BROTHER! A PIECE OF MOM.

GLAD YOU LIKE IT.

I FOUND IT IN THE LIBRARY. AND YOU'LL NEVER GUESS WHAT ELSE I FOUND-- A THESIS PAPER BY DAD!

IT BREAKS DOWN THE EGYPTIAN SOUL INTO DIFFERENT PARTS, MORE THAN JUST THE SECRET NAME AND *BA*. I THINK IF WE FIND THE SHADOW OF APOPHIS'S SOUL WE CAN...

THE SERPENT'S SHADO

A DISCOURSE ON SHEUT IN EGYPTIAN MYTHOLOGY AND ITS USES

BY

JULIUS KANE

A thesis submi
fulfil

CARTER, CAN'T WE REST FOR ONE DAY?

RIGHT, RIGHT. BUT IF YOU WANT TO DEBRIEF, THE INITIATES ARE READY.

CARTER!!

So now you know what really happened on the *equinox*.

Desjardins sacrificed his life to buy us time, but Apophis is quickly working his way out of the abyss. We may have weeks, if we're lucky, days, if we're not.

Amos has taken over the reins of Chief Lector, but some nomes are in rebellion. Many believe the Kanes have taken over by force. Amos is trying to assert himself as the leader of the House of Life, but it's not going to be easy.

Luckily, he has Zia by his side. When she's not scrying with Carter!

Ra is reborn, and once again sails the Duat night and day fighting off the process of Chaos with help from the other gods.

We're sending out the word to set the record straight.

We don't have all the answers yet. We don't know how to heal Ra, or Bes, or even Walt. We don't know what role Zia will play, or if the gods can be trusted to help us.

We don't know when or where Apophis will strike, though it'll likely be the autumn equinox.

The point is, wherever you are, whatever type of magic you practice, we need your help. Unless we unite and learn the path of the gods quickly, we don't stand a chance.

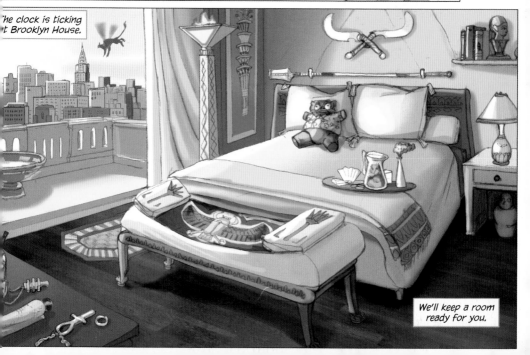

The clock is ticking at Brooklyn House.

We'll keep a room ready for you.

Adapted from the novel
The Kane Chronicles, Book Two: *The Throne of Fire*

Text copyright © 2015 by Rick Riordan
Illustrations copyright © 2015 Disney Enterprises, Inc.

Designed by Jim Titus

Printed in the United States of America
First Graphic Novel Edition, October 2015
3 5 7 9 10 8 6 4 2

FAC-008598-17362
ISBN 978-1-4847-1490-4 (hardcover)
ISBN 978-1-4847-1493-5 (paperback)

Library of Congress Control Number:
2015019210

Visit www.RickRiordan.com and www.DisneyBooks.com

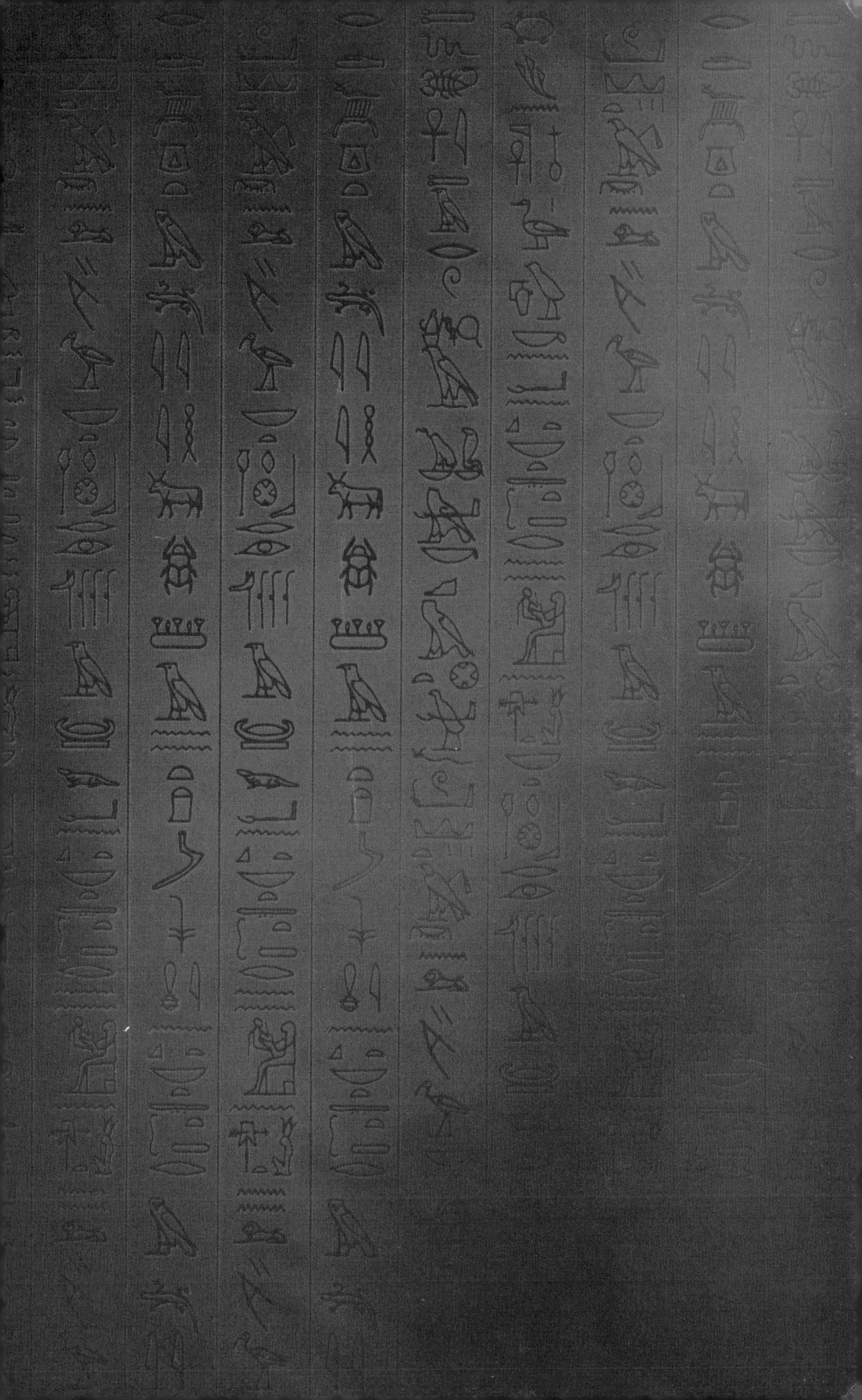